SPEED
of the
DARK

Story by
Patrick Swidler

Illustrated by
Natalie Curtiss

Speed of the Dark
by Patrick Swidler
Copyright © 2015

Illustration and Layout by
Natalie Curtiss

Published by T.K. Brown Productions
Printed in the United States of America

The text of this book is set in Economica and Josefin Sans.
The illustrations were done in acrylic on paper.

ISBN-13: 978-1514298961   ISBN-10: 1514298961

Mike studied his science and math
To show light his ultimate wrath

All day & night
He struggled with light
In hopes to get on the right path

His equations told him he couldn't
His friends would tell him he wouldn't

To prove them all wrong
Mike went along
To show he could do what he shouldn't

His dream finally came to fruition
His time to put light in submission

He gathered some speed
The people took heed
Because Mike was a man on a mission

He continued to go faster and faster
His friends could only hear laughter

Mike was a blur on his way, he was sure
To speed even light couldn't master

Mike kept going and time seemed to slow
As the fabric of space seemed to flow

He saw his own face
In an unusual place
At a time he had not yet to go

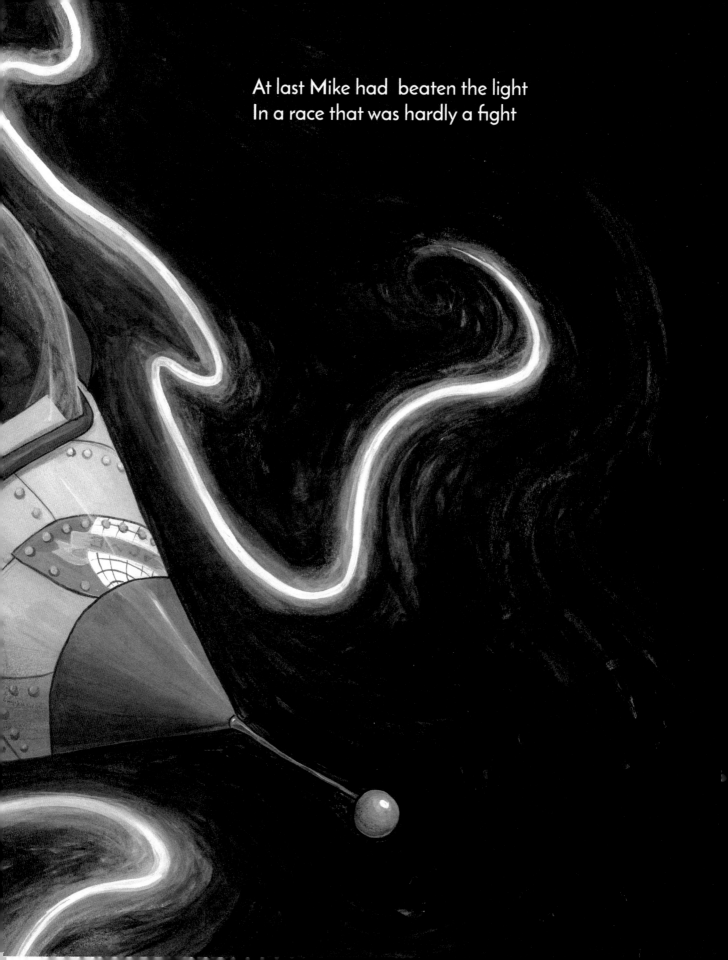

At last Mike had beaten the light
In a race that was hardly a fight

Where nothing would shine
He could travel through time
And tomorrow was the previous night

With candor and poise Mike returned
Excited to share what he'd learned

But when he finally slowed down
Something peculiar he found
His friends were all old and concerned

It had been decades since he left them they said
Each with more years behind than ahead

Mike took a moment to stare
Then wiped at a tear
And spoke of the journey he'd led

Mike described to his friends where he went
About the space and time he had bent

They were happy it seemed
He had conquered his dream
But one that he just may resent

Mike then asked his friends what he missed
About the girls and boys they first kissed

Whether life as it seemed
Through their childhood dreams
Went as well as they used to insist

Mike's friends told stories for hours
Of times both cheerful and sour

Their lives had been filled
With love and with thrills
of challenges they had to conquer

Now the night was nearing its end
But a wonderful time they did spend

As the fire grew dim
And the clock hands grew thin
Mike said goodbye to the best of his friends

He left feeling honored and pleasant
Because his journey through past and through present

Allowed him to see
What his friends came to be
And what lifelong friends really meant

At last, Mike had reached his mark
It was not quite a walk in the park

But as he gazed at the sky
With the stars in his eyes
Ok, now what is the speed of the dark?

Made in the USA
San Bernardino,
CA

57827373R00020